LITTLE
ZOO ANIMALS
COLORING BOOK

Roberta Collier

Dover Publications, Inc.
New York

Published in Canada by General Publishing Company, Ltd., 30 Lesmill Road, Don Mills, Toronto, Ontario.
Published in the United Kingdom by Constable and Company, Ltd.

Little Zoo Animals Coloring Book is a new work, first published by Dover Publications, Inc., in 1990.

DOVER *Pictorial Archive* SERIES

International Standard Book Number: 0-486-26403-3

Manufactured in the United States of America
Dover Publications, Inc., 31 East 2nd Street, Mineola, N.Y. 11501

PUBLISHER'S NOTE

In this little book you will meet lots of the same kinds of animals that you find when you visit the zoo—60 of them in all. In the pages of this book you will discover some very strange creatures indeed! A tarsier, an aardvark and a three-toed sloth are three of the animals included. And you'll also find some familiar favorites such as a sea lion, a panda, a baby elephant and a baby goat. These and 53 other animals appear in alphabetical order. They have been pictured so that you can color them in with crayons, pens or colored pencils. You can make the animals look realistic, or you can color them in any other way you want. Have fun—and happy coloring!

Aardvark

Addax

Armadillo

Baboon

Bighorn Sheep

Bison

Bobcat

Bottlenose Dolphin

Camel

17

Cape Buffalo

Caribou

Cheetah

Chimpanzee

Crested Porcupine

Eagle

Elephant

Fawn

Flamingo

Gazelle

Giraffe

Goat

Gorilla

Grizzly Bear

Hawk Owl

Hippopotamus

Kangaroo

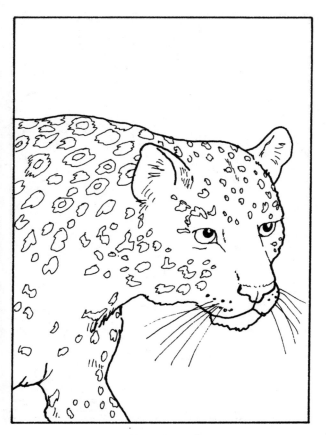

Leopard

Lion

Llama

Moose

Mountain Goat

Mountain Lion

Musk-ox

Opossum

Orangutan

Panda

Pelican

Puffin

Rabbit

Red Fox

Rhinocéros

Saki Monkey

Sea Lion

Snowy Egret

Swan

Tarsier

Three-toed Sloth

Tiger

Turtle

Vervet Monkey

Walrus

Weasel

White-tailed Deer

Wolf

Yellow Rat Snake

Zebra